THE
CHEAT

THE DO-OVER

THE
CHEAT

SARAH RICHMAN

darbycreek
MINNEAPOLIS

Darby Creek
A division of Lerner Publishing Group, Inc.
241 First Avenue North
Minneapolis, MN 55401 USA

For reading levels and more information, look up this title at www.lernerbooks.com.

Image credits: Piglon/Shutterstock.com; autsawin uttisin/Shutterstock.com; VshenZ/Shutterstock.com.

Main body text set in Janson Text LT Std 12/17.5.
Typeface provided by Adobe Systems.

Library of Congress Cataloging-in-Publication Data

Names: Richman, Sarah, author.
Title: The cheat / Sarah Richman.
Description: Minneapolis : Darby Creek, [2019] | Series: The do-over | Summary: After eighth-grader Ted decides not to join his friends in cheating on a big test and scores poorly, he gets a mysterious opportunity to relive the day and try to set things right.
Identifiers: LCCN 2018029283 (print) | LCCN 2018035956 (ebook) | ISBN 9781541541979 (eb pdf) | ISBN 9781541540347 (lb : alk. paper) | ISBN 9781541545489 (pb : alk. paper)
Subjects: | CYAC: Cheating—Fiction. | Conduct of life—Fiction. | Middle schools—Fiction. | Schools—Fiction.
Classification: LCC PZ7.1.R5333 (ebook) | LCC PZ7.1.R5333 Che 2019 (print) | DDC [Fic]—dc23
LC record available at https://lccn.loc.gov/2018029283

Manufactured in the United States of America
1 - 45239 - 36621 - 9/14/2018

FOR MY FAMILY, WHO TAUGHT ME TO LOVE
STORIES, AND FOR PETER, WHO HELPED ME
LEARN HOW TO TELL THEM. THANK YOU.

1

October was late enough in the school year for Ted to accept that summer was over, but still early enough for him to be annoyed about it. He slumped in the passenger seat of the family minivan and glowered at the backpack by his knees.

It was a Monday morning, which was bad enough, and the radio was stuck on a station playing "Monster Mash" even though Halloween was weeks away.

His mom hummed along and patted the beat on the steering wheel.

Ted did not *do* early. What he did do, quite well, was sleep. That was what he'd been doing at this time every morning during the summer, before tenth grade came around and ruined it.

Whoever it was who said change was a good thing must have been a morning person, Ted thought.

Not being a morning person, he took a few seconds to process it when, as they stopped at a red light, his mom pulled a drawing of a penguin out of her pocket.

It was a plump little penguin, a bit crumpled now, with a round belly, a snowflake electric guitar, and a Mohawk made out of icicles. Ted had drawn him on a napkin at dinner the night before. There was still a fleck of lasagna clinging to the corner of the napkin, by one of the webbed feet.

Ted stared at the penguin.

Ted's mom looked over at him. "The shading is good, kiddo."

He sighed. "Thanks."

The light turned green.

"Is this why it took you half an hour to clear the dinner table last night?" she asked.

"Maybe."

They swerved slightly to avoid a pothole, making their way toward school.

"I love the way you draw, Teddy, you know I do." His mom pushed a wisp of hair behind her ear. "I'm just hoping that you will spend a little more time on other things too."

Like my grades, Ted thought.

"Like your grades," she continued. She flicked the turn signal. "You'll need good grades when you start to apply for college scholarships, and it's never too early to start standing out."

Ted opened his mouth to respond but then closed it. Unless there was a college scholarship for doodling or for sleeping until noon, standing out wasn't exactly on the table, but he wasn't going to push the point.

They rolled up to the front of the Thomas T. Tenley High School, a squat one-story building held up in the front by a set of blue columns and held up everywhere else by pure will. The last renovation, Ted's friend Adam liked to say, had been in the ugly Stone Age.

Adam and Jenn were waiting for him out

by the bike rack at the main entrance. Jenn, who was on the school's undefeated girls' soccer team, held a pair of purple cleats in one hand and a bagel in the other. Adam, a whiz at the piano and most video games—he had the second-highest *Robo-Gorilla Showdown* score in the whole state—was doing something on his phone.

The three of them had been friends since third grade, and Ted knew that when it came to scholarships, Adam and Jenn would stand out without question. They were better at music and soccer, respectively, than he was at drawing on napkins. Or anything. He didn't quite know why they kept him around, but he was glad that they did.

Ted leaned over and gave his mom a quick kiss on the cheek. "I'm sorry. I'll try, Mom. Thanks for the ride."

The car behind them beeped.

"All right already, enough!" his mom snapped into the rearview mirror. "Not you, Teddy. Have a good day."

"You too."

Ted slid out of the minivan and closed the door behind him.

His mom waved and drove away.

* * *

"Sup, Ted?" said Jenn, finishing a bite of her bagel as Ted walked up to them.

Adam slid his phone back into his jacket pocket and grinned. "You've got some major Ted-Head going on there. Have some *shame*."

"Don't kid yourself," Ted said with a chuckle. "People would drive miles to see this hair."

"People would drive miles *away* from that hair," said Jenn. "Come here." She handed the cleats and the bagel to Adam. "If you finish my bagel, Adam, you're dead to me."

"It's a risk I'm willing to take," he replied, taking a small bite.

Jenn patted down the top of Ted's head. "Okay, it's a bit better. Now we can be seen with you."

"Thanks," said Ted.

"Yeah, Nina Alvarez is going to take one

look at you and fall deeply in love," said Adam as he passed back Jenn's things.

Fine by me, thought Ted.

The warning bell for first period classes rang.

Jenn stuffed the rest of her bagel in her mouth. "All right," she said in a muffled voice. "History class, here we come."

* * *

By some scheduling miracle, Ted, Jenn, and Adam had all been placed in the same first-period history class. They sat close enough to the front to hear what Ms. Stevenson was saying but far back enough to goof off. That had been Jenn's idea. She had desk picking down to a science.

Back here, Ted could also see the back of Nina Alvarez's head, which was also a plus. Getting to look at Nina's neck and sometimes her left ear when she turned to talk to somebody was one of the only things that made first period tolerable.

Ted hadn't worked up the nerve to actually

talk to her yet, but he was getting there. He was *getting to* getting there, anyway.

"Good morning, everyone! I hope you all had a fun weekend." Ms. Stevenson beamed from the front of the room. She always said *good morning* like she meant it.

"We ended last week's class by talking about what life was like for mining families who moved west during the California gold rush," Ms. Stevenson said, handing an armful of worksheet packets to each of the students in the front row. "Take one and pass the rest down, thanks. Today," she continued over the rustling sound of the papers, "we're going to take a closer look at how the California gold rush changed the lives of the people who were already living in the area."

"Five bucks says that this is going to put us all to sleep," murmured Jenn.

"No deal," said Ted.

"Good call," whispered Adam.

"Want to play tic-tac-toe?" Jenn drew a large hashtag on the corner of her worksheet packet. "Bet you can't beat me."

Ted nodded, trying to keep listening to Ms. Stevenson, who was now reading a super sad letter from a dead guy out loud. He reached over and drew a small circle in the corner space.

Fourteen games of tic-tac-toe and four worksheets later, Ms. Stevenson checked her watch. "Okay everyone, let's stop here. I have an announcement."

The clock on the wall, just past Nina's neck, showed five minutes left in class.

Ms. Stevenson cleared her throat. "The California gold rush unit test will be held this Wednesday."

Jenn dropped her pencil.

Nina raised her hand.

Even the way she raises her hand is perfect, thought Ted.

"Yes, Nina?"

"What will the test format be, Ms. Stevenson?"

"Great question! The test will be fifty multiple choice questions," she replied, picking up another crisp stack of papers. "They will all be about what we've learned these last few weeks in class and in the textbook readings. This study guide will list what you will need to know, but everything should already be in your notes."

Ted's stomach lurched. He looked down at his sparse notes, covered in tic-tac-toe games and a drawing of a pumpkin in a prospector's hat.

This is not good, he thought.

Ted pictured the look on his mom's face when he would bring this unit test home, covered in red ink and failure, letting her down again.

Behind him, he heard Adam groan.

"I have that big piano recital on Thursday night. How am I supposed to practice enough if I have this thing to study for instead?"

"Yeah, and I have that soccer game on Saturday," Jenn hissed. "We're playing Melville High. If I mess up our team's winning streak because I'm sitting around studying instead of doing drills, our coach is going to kill me."

"My notes stink," Ted murmured. "It's too bad that there's no way to go back and get all of the answers."

The bell rang, ending class.

"Don't forget to grab a copy of the study guide on your way out," called Ms. Stevenson, "and to have a great rest of your Monday! Go Tenley Toads!"

* * *

Ted came home from school and tried to delay the inevitable by watching game show reruns until dinner, ignoring the tingling in his chest and the study guide in his backpack.

At dinner, he slowly chewed his meatloaf and listened to his mom talk about work.

After the dishes were cleared, though, Ted knew that he couldn't put off studying any longer. He excused himself and went up to his room, closing the door to muffle the sound of the TV downstairs.

Time to get to work, he thought.

Ted's desk had always been more shelf than desk—a pine-colored plastic surface for plates, comic books, markers, and papers to sit until he got around to dealing with them. He pushed everything to the side and laid out his history textbook, his study guide, and his notes.

I can do this, Ted thought. *I can totally do this.*

He ran his hands through his hair and exhaled slowly.

"Okay," he whispered to himself. "From the top."

Ted looked at the terms at the top of the study guide, letting his pencil tap against the paper, leaving tiny flecks of graphite on the page.

Uh, maybe from the bottom.

Ted flipped to the end of the study guide and sighed. No luck there either. He could recall Ms. Stevenson talking about some of the terms, but the details were fuzzy—too fuzzy. He drew a brain on the edge of the study guide, lying on a head-shaped couch and talking to a long, blobby alien with a notepad.

What else do you remember? he wrote in a speech bubble above the alien's head.

Ted traced another speech bubble above the brain.

I really can't say, said the brain.

It was going to be a long night.

2

Tuesday started off pitch black. Something was pressed against Ted's face. He blinked, eyelashes scraping paper, and realized that he had fallen asleep face-first in his history notes.

Ted sat up, rubbing his sore neck. Light was just beginning to shine through the window shade.

Maybe I still have time to go back to sleep for a little bit, he thought.

Right on cue, his alarm went off.

"Ugghhh."

He threw on some clothes that smelled clean enough and trudged over to the bathroom, the old wood floor in the hall squeaking in protest under his feet.

You and me both, buddy, Ted thought.

He splashed cool water on his face, brushed his teeth, retrieved his backpack, and went downstairs to meet his mom by the front door.

"Did you get breakfast, Teddy?" she asked, putting on a swipe of pink lipstick in the small entryway mirror.

Ted shook his head. "Nope. No time."

"Go grab an apple from the kitchen," said his mom, clicking the lipstick closed. "You can eat it on the way."

Apple in hand, he climbed into the minivan a moment later.

His mom held the steering wheel with one hand and patted at a wrinkle in her dress with the other. "Shoot. I must have missed this one with the iron. How obvious is it?"

Ted squinted over at her. "I can tell that the dress is wrinkled, but it's not too bad."

She sighed. "Thanks, kiddo." She started the engine and began to pull out of the driveway.

Ted let his eyes close and his head lean

against the seat cover. He felt floppy, as if someone had let the air out of him.

"Just so you know," his mom said, "I'm going to have meetings all day tomorrow, starting pretty early in the day."

"Earlier than *this*?" asked Ted.

She shook her head. "You don't even want to know what time it starts."

"When?"

"No."

"Tell me."

"Five thirty."

"Gross!"

She laughed, pausing to let a mail truck pass them. "Gross indeed. I'm telling you now because it means I won't be able to drive you to school tomorrow or to pick you up afterward. You'll need to take the bus."

Ted grunted in acknowledgement.

"I'll leave a reminder note and some money on the kitchen table."

"Thanks, Mom."

* * *

The rest of Tuesday morning went by in a haze—try to pay attention, doze off, try to pay attention, doodle, and repeat. By the time Ted felt almost awake, it was already lunch. He was sitting against a locker in the math wing of the school, holding a roast beef sandwich halfway between his face and his lap.

"You in, Ted?"

Ted looked up from his sandwich.

Jenn and Adam were both staring at him.

"Sorry, what?"

"After Adam's piano recital on Thursday night," Jenn repeated, "a bunch of us are probably going to the diner for burgers and shakes. Are you in?"

"Oh, yeah," said Ted, putting the sandwich down. "I have to check with my mom first, but count me in."

Jenn frowned. "Are you all right? You seem really out of it today."

"Yeah, real 'Night of the Living Ted' material," Adam joked, scooping more salsa onto a tortilla chip. "You alive?"

"Just tired, that's all. Tomorrow's history

test is really messing with me," Ted admitted. He ran a hand through his hair. "I tried studying for it last night and fell asleep in my notes."

"At least you got to study," said Jenn. "Soccer practice ran late last night and I had a science project due today."

They both turned to Adam, who had a strange smile on his face.

Jenn put her orange juice down. "What's that look about?"

Adam put his hands together. "What if I told you guys that you didn't need to study for the test?"

Ted felt goose bumps up and down his arms. "What do you mean?"

Adam arched an eyebrow. "I mean, Teddy Bear, that something glorious has happened." He looked up and down the hallway and lowered his voice. "You know how the pencil sharpener in the history room is right by Ms. Stevenson's desk, and how my dad always buys me those awful old-fashioned, off-brand pencils that I have to spend ages sharpening?

"Well, I was sharpening my pencil in

history class this morning," Adam continued as soon as the juniors were out of earshot, "and I noticed that good old Ms. Stevenson left her purse open on the floor next to her desk. Sticking out of it was—"

"Oh my god," Jenn said in a hushed voice.

"The answer key to tomorrow's unit test," said Adam, grinning. He took a swig of his soda, smacking his lips.

Jenn tilted her head back against the wall of lockers, watching him. "Did you do what I think you did?"

Ted held his breath.

Adam laughed. "I did." He fished his cell phone out of his pocket, tapped on the screen, and held it up for them to see. "Lady and gentleman, I present to you a picture of the answer key."

"You evil genius," squealed Jenn, clasping her hands together. "You're officially my favorite person. Text it to me!"

"Coming right up," said Adam. "Ted, do you want it too?"

Ted swallowed. "I . . . I don't know."

"What do you mean you don't know?" demanded Jenn.

"Isn't that, uh . . ." Ted paused, feeling clammy in his sweatshirt. "Cheating?"

"I mean, technically, yes," said Adam. "But I like to think of it as a shortcut to your grade. You could get there the long way, by spending the rest of tonight studying, or you could get there the short way with the answer key."

"Also, my mom says that tests and grades can't capture the human spirit," Jenn added.

"Yeah, that too," said Adam. "Besides, it's kind of Ms. Stevenson's fault for leaving the answer key visible like that." He frowned down at his phone. "The service is terrible down here. My text isn't going through. I'll just write them out for you later, Jenn. I was going to make a paper cheat sheet for myself anyway. If I make them small enough, we can fold them up in the palms of our hands to sneak into the test."

"Amazing," said Jenn. "Thank you!"

"No sweat," Adam replied.

Ted wiped at his sticky forehead. "Aren't you guys worried about getting in trouble?"

Jenn rolled her eyes. "If Ms. Stevenson didn't notice that the answers were sticking out of her bag, do you think she'll notice anything else? Besides, what she doesn't know can't hurt her."

The bell rang again, ending lunch.

"Look, Ted, we're not going to make you take the answers," said Adam. "It's up to you." He stood up.

Ted took a deep breath and smiled thinly up at him. "I think I'm going to pass. Thanks, though."

Adam shrugged. "Your loss, dude." He turned to Jenn. "Ready for Spanish?"

Jenn nodded. She stood and swung her backpack onto one shoulder. "See you, Ted."

Ted stayed where he was sitting and watched them walk away. He looked down, realizing he was still holding his roast beef sandwich. He wasn't even hungry anymore. *Guess I'll be studying on my own for this one*, he thought.

* * *

Ted sat in a third-row desk in English class, next to a pair of theater kids, Fred and Rosie.

They were too busy comparing their notes in the margins of *The Tragedy of Romeo and Juliet* to care that Ted wasn't contributing to the group activity again.

"I'm just saying, I think that Juliet's mom would have picked up on that here," said Fred.

"Lady Capulet had no idea what she was dealing with," Rosie shot back. "You can't expect her to see what the audience sees."

Fred rolled his eyes.

If I cheated on that test, thought Ted, *would my mom be able to tell? Would Ms. Stevenson?*

In his notebook, Ted drew a stick figure woman with a wrinkled dress, like his mom's, and two arching lines for arms flung up in a shrug as if to say, *"You tell me, kiddo."*

He added two circles and a line to her face, giving his drawing a pair of glasses. He went to add dots for her eyes but then hesitated, his pencil hovering above the paper.

It didn't matter. He had made a good call by not taking the answers. It would have been the wrong thing to do. Ted knew that, even as he pictured the history test sitting blankly in front of him the next morning, on a desk just like this one. He had made the right choice.

Right?

"Either way, it ends badly," Ted mumbled.

"It sure does," said Fred, flipping through the pages of the play.

* * *

That night, Ted sat at his desk again and stared down at his study guide, history textbook, and notes. He'd hoped that, somehow, everything he needed for the test tomorrow was just stuck in his brain and that by now some of it would have shaken loose.

It hadn't. Ted sighed and rubbed his neck, feeling just as unprepared as he had the day before. Ted didn't know much about the California gold rush, but he did know two things for sure: he wasn't ready for this test, and he was running out of time.

3

Ted woke up the next morning to his radio alarm clock with the volume cranked all the way up.

"Good morning, listeners!" said the DJ. "That song was "Monster Mash" by Bobby Pickett. Get ready for two more October favorites, Michael Jackson's "Thriller" and "Time Warp" from *The Rocky Horror Picture Show!*"

"Not today," said Ted.

He smacked his hand down on top of the alarm clock, felt for the off button, then threw on some clothes and shuffled downstairs.

Good morning, Teddy! read the note on the kitchen table. *Just a reminder that I am at an early meeting, and I won't be able to drive you to school or pick you up afterward. Here's some money for the bus.*

Ted slowly worked through a mouthful of toast, squinting down at his mom's handwriting.

P.S., it's Wednesday, and you know what that means.

He groaned. It was test day.

Trash day, his mom's note continued. *Please bring the trash cans to the curb when you get home from school.*

Ted crumpled up the note and threw it into the recycling bin. Trash cans were not something he could think about right now. That was for After-School-Ted. Right now, Before-School-Ted had a bigger issue at hand: the test. Specifically, getting to it.

He swallowed his toast, grabbed his bus fare and his backpack, opened the front door, and stepped out into the October air.

* * *

The number 42 bus stopped just a couple of blocks from Ted's house every twenty minutes according to the schedule posted online.

Come on, Bus, Ted thought.

He pulled the strings of his sweatshirt tighter around his chin, switching between glaring at his flashcards and glaring at the cross-street where the bus was supposed to appear, any minute now.

Don't do this to me today.

Ted checked the time on his phone—the bus should have been there three minutes ago.

He began to pace.

Finally, he heard the rumble of the bus. It inched up to the stop, and after what felt like eight years, the green-and-yellow door swung open.

"Hold up there, son," said the bus driver. "There's a passenger coming out."

Ted's eyes bulged.

"I'm sorry, dear," an old lady called from just inside the bus. "I'll just be a moment . . . I'm not moving so fast today. It's the hips, you see, they want to stay on the bus."

"Take your time, Millie," said the driver.

Something clattered and fell.

"Whoops! Don't mind me, that's just the

cane . . . do you mind—oh thank you, ma'am, you are too kind." The old lady hoisted herself and her cane down to the sidewalk. "Thank you for your patience, young man."

Ted forced a smile on his face. "No problem."

He climbed aboard, paid the bus fare, and found an empty seat by the window.

Finally.

The bus lurched forward and then stopped.

Ted peered out the window and saw that a trash truck had pulled in front of the bus. "Trash day," he whispered, remembering his mom's note. He watched as two workers hopped off of the truck and slowly picked up each trash can along the street, one at a time, before spinning like dancers in the world's slowest and smelliest dance and dumping the contents into the truck.

"Sorry, folks," the bus driver called. "Looks like we'll be running a few extra minutes behind schedule."

* * *

The bus reached Ted's stop twenty minutes after class started. He flew off the bus and across the Thomas T. Tenley High School parking lot, slamming one foot in front of the other. His backpack slapped limply against his back.

Was this parking lot always so long?

He reached the blue double doors and burst through them in a blaze of sweat and panic.

"No running," called a hall monitor.

Ted ran past him.

He stumbled down a staircase, turned a corner, slid down the hall, and lunged at the door to his history classroom. The doorknob turned and Ted half walked, half fell into the room.

His classmates all looked up at him from their tests.

"Welcome!" chirped Ms. Stevenson from behind her desk. "We've already started, but you're not too far behind."

She held out a blank test. "Here you go!"

"Thanks."

The test trembled a bit in Ted's hands as he walked down the row of desks to his seat.

Adam's face looked smooth and calm as he looked down at his test.

Jenn was smiling slightly as she worked on hers.

Can I even call that work? Ted wondered as he sat down. *They're just pretending to do what I'm about to actually do.* His heart was still pounding from the run. *Okay. Ignore it, Ted. Just focus.*

When Ted looked down at his test, though, the writing seemed to wobble on the page. He read the first question three times before the letters behaved themselves and settled into words.

What impact did President James K. Polk's comments to Congress in 1848 have on the California gold rush?

Ted tapped his pencil against his temple. He remembered Ms. Stevenson talking about President Polk. It had sounded like "President Poke," and he had drawn hedgehogs in button-down shirts all over his notes that day. Ted could picture the hedgehogs, just not the information that he had written next to them.

Out of the corner of his eye, Ted saw Jenn calmly turn a page on her test.

He put a star next to the first question and skipped to the second question.

What were the three main routes that people used to reach California?

Ted narrowed the five answer options down to three, but then he got stuck again. He drew another star and moved to the third question.

Soon the first two pages of the test were covered in stars like a constellation of doubt.

Adam had taught him a test-taking strategy he'd named "Preemptive Panic." You starred all of the test questions you weren't sure about, added them all up, and subtracted that number from the total number of test questions to see what your worst possible score could be. That way you could be prepared for the worst and get a somewhat happy surprise if you guessed some answers correctly.

So far, only nine questions were starless. His paper looked like the kind of night sky that people see out in the countryside or in the desert.

Behind him, he heard the scrape of Adam's chair being pushed back.

Adam strolled up to the front of the room, his backpack slung over one shoulder, and handed his test to Ms. Stevenson.

"That was fast, Adam! You weren't rushing your California gold rush test, were you?"

A couple of students chuckled quietly.

"I wouldn't dream of it, Ms. S," said Adam. "Could I please leave early, since I'm done?"

Ms. Stevenson smiled. "Of course. Have a great rest of your Wednesday!" She took a look at her watch. "We still have about fifteen minutes left for the rest of you to finish. Take your time!"

I am, thought Ted. *That's the problem.*

He looked back at his test paper.

Who was Samuel Brannan?

On the corner of his test, Ted drew a large question mark wearing a cowboy hat and boots with little spurs.

Jenn slowly flipped her test to the front page, picked up her bag, and headed to the front of the room.

Ted watched her hand Mrs. Stevenson her test and walk out the door to join Adam in the hall. Before the door closed, he caught a glimpse of them high-fiving.

One by one, the rest of his classmates finished their tests and filtered out of the door. The stack of tests on Ms. Stevenson's desk grew taller and taller.

Soon, Ted was the last one left.

At five minutes before the bell, Ms. Stevenson gave a polite cough. At two minutes before the bell, she said kindly, "Ted, you're just about out of time."

Ted wiped the sweat off of his upper lip and nodded. He circled random letters for the last eight answers and then admitted defeat. He shoved his pencil back into his backpack, stood, and handed his damp test paper to Ms. Stevenson just as the bell rang.

* * *

Ted couldn't focus in any of his other classes. He buzzed with a nervous energy that he just couldn't shake, even after running laps in second-period gym class. For the rest of the day, he just kept doodling little boxes on everything, as if he could climb right in and forget about what a disaster that test was.

Maybe I should have just cheated with Adam and Jenn, he thought as his science class talked about genes

"This," his science teacher said, pointing to a slide with a sour-looking guy on it, "is August Weismann. Some people used to think that if you got a major injury, you could pass it on to your kids. August did an experiment to prove them wrong. He took some mice and cut off their tails, and then waited to see if their babies would be born with shorter tails or no tails at all."

He clicked to the next slide, showing a picture of some mice. Their tails were, as far as Ted could tell, normal.

"As you can see, that's not how life works. Even if you lose your tail, the next generation gets to start over."

Ted drew another little box on his notes. Starting over sounded nice.

His pocket vibrated; Adam had texted their group chat.

> I think Nina's coming to the diner with all of us
> after my recital tomorrow night . . .

Ted's heart did a running jump into his throat. He had somehow forgotten that Nina also played piano.

Jenn sent a heart eyes emoji.

> OMG. Ted can finally make his move!

Adam instantly responded.

> Yes! Get her number, dude! Be her Ted in
> Shining Armor!

Ted checked that the coast was still clear and then quickly texted them back.

> If my mom even lets me out of the house
> when she sees what I got on that test . . .
> maybe. LOL.

Adam sent a GIF of a baby giving a thumbs-up.

Jenn, this random baby, and I all believe in you.

Ted tried and failed to tune back in to what his teacher was saying. He had been flustered before; now he was doubly flustered.

He imagined casually sliding into the diner booth next to Nina. She wouldn't be able to decide between a chocolate milkshake or a vanilla milkshake. He would offer to get one and she could get the other. They would share—two straws in each milkshake.

Of course, none of that would happen if his mom made him stay home because he failed that test. It would all come down to his grade.

Who knows, maybe I'm a lucky guesser, Ted mused.

He slid his phone back into his pocket and waited for the bell to ring. The sooner Wednesday ended, the sooner he would get his test back—the sooner he would know.

4

The next day, Ted held his breath as Ms. Stevenson walked through the rows of desks, handing back the graded tests one by one. The only thing scarier than test day was the day that you got your test back. The only thing scarier than *that* was knowing that your grade could make or break your social life.

No pressure, thought Ted.

He watched his classmates' faces as they saw their grades.

Over her shoulder, Ted could see that Nina had gotten 50 out of 50. He wasn't surprised. She was good at everything.

Jenn let out a happy whoop. "I got a forty-nine! Not bad."

Adam gave her a high five. "Same. What are the odds?" He lowered his voice. "I must have misread number eighteen when I copied the answers from the picture. Sorry about that."

"Hey, no complaints here," Jenn said with a shrug. "What did you end up getting, Ted?"

Ted looked down at his test paper, still facedown on his desk. "To be honest, I haven't looked."

"I could look for you, if you want," Adam offered.

Ted nodded and passed him his test. Inside, his stomach was doing an unhappy version of the conga. He watched Adam's face, trying not to look at the reflection of his test in Adam's glasses.

Adam's nostril's flared slightly.

Oh no.

"How bad is it?" Ted asked.

Adam paused, and then cleared his throat. "It's, uh, not your finest work."

Jenn grabbed the test from Adam. Her eyes

widened. "Oh, Ted," she murmured.

Ted grabbed the test from Jenn.

Oh, Ted, he thought.

He had gotten a 17 out of 50. Ted had never realized how much he disliked looking at the numbers one and seven. The number one was just a scratch on the page—lazy. There was no imagination to that one. Next to it, the number seven just looked like a failed triangle.

No, he thought. *It's me. I'm the failed triangle.*

"Hey, cheer up," said Adam. "It could have been worse."

Ted put his face down on his desk. The fake plastic wood was cool and comforting against his forehead.

"Adam, he's face-planting," said Jenn.

In Ted's mind, what was supposed to be his first interaction with Nina at the diner that night warped and blurred, like that one time when he tried on Adam's glasses.

"Incoming," hissed Adam.

Ted heard footsteps, and then he could smell Ms. Stevenson's perfume—something with flowers—somewhere close by. He straightened up to see Ms. Stevenson standing over his desk, looking concerned.

"Ted, are you all right?"

Behind Ms. Stevenson, Ted saw Nina raise her eyebrows.

"I'm fine," said Ted, "just, um, tired."

"Okay." Ms. Stevenson fixed her brown eyes on his. "Just so you know," she said quietly, "if you are ever interested in coming by at lunch to go over this test, my door is always open."

Ted swallowed. "Thanks. I might take you up on that."

Ms. Stevenson smiled. "Glad to hear it."

The bell rang.

Ted shoved the graded test deep into his backpack and followed Jenn and Adam out of the classroom.

They headed over to Jenn's locker, dodging a janitor pushing a mop and a wheeled bucket toward the bathroom down the hall.

"I can't believe that worked, Adam," said Jenn, twisting her combination into the lock and pulling the locker door open.

"It's amazing what you can do when luck meets laziness," Adam replied.

"Just out of curiosity," said Ted, "how did you do it?" He paused. "The cheating, I mean."

Jenn whipped around, soccer bag in hand. "Shush!"

"Relax," said Adam. "Nobody's listening." He slipped his hand into his jeans pocket and pulled out a small strip of paper. "I wrote mine on here."

"I made one of those too," said Jenn, "but I also had a backup." She tugged up her shirtsleeve, revealing three faint rows of letters written on her skin. "My soccer tan came in handy. Less contrast."

"That's awesome," said Adam. He gave Ted a playful nudge in the side. "Good thing you didn't try that, Ted. Ms. Stevenson would have seen that from a mile away."

"Maybe," Ted replied. "Or maybe I would have gotten better than a seventeen out of fifty. My mom is going to be so mad."

"Hey," said Adam, "maybe she won't care! You should just tell her. You never know, dude."

Jenn closed her locker door and turned the lock. "I know you're bummed right now, so I'm not going to say we told you so. Just know that I am thinking it."

"She's nicer than I am," teased Adam. "We told you so. You totally should have cheat—"

Jenn smacked him on the arm.

"Hey!"

Ted snorted. "Thanks, guys."

Maybe I should have, he thought.

* * *

There is never a good time to tell your mom that you failed a test right after she asked you to try harder in school, so Ted told his mom at dinner, halfway through a bite of chicken salad.

She put her fork down. "You got a what out of fifty?"

Ted swallowed his food and repeated himself.

"Ted, kiddo, we just talked about putting more effort into your grades."

"I know. I'm sorry. I—"

"No," his mom said, interrupting him. "I'm

sorry. I should have been stricter with you. Dancing around this clearly did not work."

"Mom, it's not about that at all," said Ted. "I did try. I'm just really bad at this, all right?" He picked up his plate. "Look, can we just wait and talk about this after I come home from Adam's recital and the diner?"

"No," said his mom. "You are not going out to Adam's recital or the diner tonight. You are going to stay here and you are going to spend some time with your other schoolwork."

"But Mom, I already told Adam and Jenn that I would go. And there's this girl I wanted to see tonight—"

His mom shook her head. "No, Teddy. Your friends and your drawing have clearly been too much of a distraction for you. I know I've never done this before, but seventeen out of fifty is just not okay. You're . . . what's the word?"

"Grounded?" Ted asked.

"Grounded. Yeah. That's it. You're grounded."

* * *

Ted closed his bedroom door behind him, flicked off the lights, and flopped onto his bed. He pulled his phone out of his pocket and sent Jenn and Adam a text in their group chat.

Grounded. Stuck here tonight. She is
so mad . . .

He let the phone drop onto his bedspread and stared up at the blotchy water stain on his ceiling. It looked like one of those blob fish from the nature channel.

Ted's phone buzzed with messages from Adam. In the dark, they lit up the screen, one after another.

Dude. Seriously? Tonight's the recital. Are you
really not coming? You know I get nervous
up there!

Jenn joined in, sending a poop emoji.

That's what it's going to feel like sitting next
to your empty seat tonight, Ted. Don't bail on

him. Or me! And what about Nina? Tonight
could be your chance!

Ted felt like his thumbs were moving
through butter as he typed back.

I'm sorry, guys. I really am.

He watched Adam type, stop, retype, and
stop again.

K. Fine. See you later, Jenn.

Jenn sent back a thumbs-up emoji, and then
Ted's screen went dark again.

No more texts—just Ted's heartbeat
punching into his ribs, and the blob fish water
stain on the ceiling.

Great, he thought. *Now everyone is mad at me.*

Ted usually looked forward to Fridays, but
tomorrow was going to stink—everything
from an awkward car ride with his mom to
Adam and Jenn most likely ignoring him.
And he'd still be stuck admiring Nina from

afar since he'd miss his chance to talk to her at the diner.

Ted yanked one of the pillows off of the bed and threw it across the floor, hoping it would make him feel better.

It didn't. Ted stared at the pillow on his floor, a sad lump of cotton and feathers, and felt like the loneliest person in the world.

I wish I had cheated with them after all, he thought. *None of this would have happened.*

That's when Ted's phone made a funny little bleep noise, one that he hadn't heard before.

That's weird, he thought. *I always keep my phone on vibrate.*

Ted squinted down at text message on the screen.

Would you like to have a do-over? Reply with YES or NO.

It wasn't in the group chat. It wasn't from Adam or Jenn at all. The message looked like it was from an unknown number.

A do-over, thought Ted. *Wouldn't that be nice?*

Ted yawned. The text made no sense, but his eyes were probably just tired from the long day. In fact, all of him was tired. Through half-closed eyes, Ted watched his thumb slowly flick the letters *y*, *e*, and *s* into the reply box. He hit the send button, rolled over, and let himself fade into sleep.

◀◀

5

Ted's radio alarm clock woke him up at
maximum volume again.

"Good morning, listeners!" said the DJ.
"That song was "Monster Mash" by Bobby
Pickett. Get ready for two more October
favorites, Michael Jackson's "Thriller" and "Time
Warp" from *The Rocky Horror Picture Show!*"

Ted groaned and reached for the off button.
The radio stations in town were getting so
repetitive. "There are other songs," he muttered.

He got dressed and went downstairs. "Mom?"

The house was quiet.

That's weird, he thought.

His mom was probably still mad at

him, but it wasn't like her to give him the silent treatment.

Ted headed into the kitchen and noticed another note and more spare change on the kitchen table.

That's . . . also weird.

It looked just like the note that his mom had left for him two days before. He picked it up for a closer look.

Good morning, Teddy! read the note. *Just a reminder that I am at an early meeting, and I won't be able to drive you to school or pick you up afterward. Here's some money for the bus.*

Ted frowned.

P.S., it's Wednesday, and you know what that means. Trash day. Please bring the trash cans to the curb when you get home from school.

Ted let his mom's note drop to the table. It had been Thursday when he had gone to bed the night before—it was supposed to be Friday now. This had to be some sort of mistake, or a prank. Then again, Ted didn't see his mom as the pranking type. This just didn't make sense.

He pulled out his phone and checked the

date: Wednesday. He went over to the tear-off calendar by the fruit bowl: Wednesday. He went to the computer in his mom's home office: Wednesday. He ran upstairs and checked the screen on his radio alarm clock: Wednesday.

Is this really happening?

Then Ted remembered the do-over text. He pulled out his phone again and looked through his messages. There was nothing in his inbox from the day before, including the mysterious text, but he knew he wasn't just making it up. It was if all the evidence that yesterday had actually happened had disappeared.

Ted sank down to sit on the edge of his bed, processing. Somehow, he really had gotten a do-over of Wednesday.

Man, thought Ted, *this makes me wish that I played the lottery. If I knew what today's numbers were, I could buy a million cheeseburgers or a car.*

Then he stood up. He couldn't use his do-over to win the lottery, but he could redo everything about the California gold rush test. If he had just said yes to Adam's offer, he wouldn't have failed. His mom wouldn't have grounded

him. Nobody would be angry with him, his
grades would bounce back, and he would be able
to go to the diner after Adam's recital and finally
make some progress with Nina.

Ted grinned. He didn't understand why
or how, but he had gotten a certified second
chance. His Wednesday didn't have to be
awful. This time, it was going to be awesome.

He got up and bounded down the stairs.
This time, Ted left the bus fare on the table.
He wasn't going to go through that mess again.

He went around to the shed behind his
house and pulled out his bike instead. The
dents in the turquoise metal glinted in the
October sun. There was still almost enough
air in the tires. It was perfect.

He strapped on his helmet, kicked out the
kickstand, and pedaled off in the direction of
Thomas T. Tenley High School.

* * *

Without a trash truck or traffic in the way this
time, Ted made it to school in record time.
Inside, he found Jenn leaning against her locker.

She finished the text she was typing on her phone, looked up at him, and smiled. "Hey, you."

"Hi," Ted replied. "Do you, uh, know where Adam is?"

"He's in the music room," said Jenn. "I think he's getting in some extra practice time on the piano before the recital tomorrow night."

Shoot, thought Ted.

"How did studying for the test go last night?"

It took Ted a second to remember that her last night was his three nights ago.

"Not my best," he admitted. "That's actually what I wanted to talk to Adam about."

Jenn tilted her head. "Oh yeah?"

"Yeah." Ted let his voice drop to a whisper. "I changed my mind about . . . you know. The test. I want in. I want," he paused, "to cheat."

"Are you sure, Ted? I mean, you seemed pretty against it yesterday."

He nodded. "I'm sure."

Jenn checked the time on her phone. "Okay, you still have time. You can look at the cheat sheet Adam made for me. I would offer to just give it to you, but I think the answers that I wrote on my arm got smeared. Take this"—she dug a small piece of paper out of her pocket—"and go copy it in the bathroom where no one can see you."

Ted grabbed the paper before he could change his mind. "Okay."

In the bathroom, Ted hurried into an empty stall, locked it, and unfurled the cheat sheet.

Wow, he thought. *Adam's handwriting is tiny.*

He had somehow fit all fifty answers in three small, neat rows. Ted took out a pen and copied them all down as fast as he could.

When he got back out to the hallway by Jenn's locker, Adam was standing there with Jenn, waiting for him.

He gave Ted a friendly slap on the back. "I hear you'll be joining us, buddy!"

Ted gave a sheepish shrug. "Yeah. I changed my mind." He handed Jenn her cheat sheet. "Thanks for letting me copy yours."

"No problem."

The bell rang and students started streaming in the direction of their first-period class.

Let's do this, thought Ted.

He pressed his cheat sheet into his palm, took a slow breath, and entered the history classroom behind his friends. He felt like an actor walking onstage. His role: Ted, taker of tests.

The performance of a lifetime, he thought.

Ms. Stevenson handed out the California gold rush test papers.

"Just bring these up to the front when you're done," she said to the class. "You may begin. Good luck, everyone!"

With that small scrap of paper tucked into his hand, Ted didn't need luck. He felt almost giddy as he matched up the answers to the questions.

What impact did President James K. Polk's comments to Congress in 1848 have on the California gold rush?

The answer was *A: Polk confirmed that there was gold in California, inspiring more people to travel there to find it.*

What were the three main routes people used to reach California?

The answer was *D: Around Cape Horn,*

through the Panama Canal, and across the Oregon Trail.

Who was Samuel Brannan?

The answer was *B: "Gold Fever" promoter and California's first millionaire.*

It was stunningly easy. All he had to do was take a peek at the cheat sheet in his hand, memorize the letters for the next five or six answers, and then pretend he was actually mulling over which letter to choose.

Adam finished his test first again. He put on one strap of his backpack and handed his test paper to Ms. Stevenson.

"That was fast, Adam! You weren't rushing your California gold rush test, were you?" said Ms. Stevenson, just like she had the first time.

Ted looked back down at his test, hiding a grin.

"Wouldn't dream of it, Ms. S," said Adam. "Could I please leave early, since I'm done?"

"Of course," Ms. Stevenson replied. "Have a great rest of your Wednesday!" She took a look at her watch, just like she had before. "We still have about fifteen minutes left for the rest of you to finish. Take your time!"

Ted waited for Jenn to get up and turn her test in early as well.

After Jenn went out into the hall again, Ted counted to thirty in his head, and then he stood up too. He gathered his things, headed up the aisle of desks, and gave his test to Ms. Stevenson.

"I'm done too," he said, trying to keep his voice casual. "Do you, um, mind if I also step out?"

"Not a problem, Ted," Ms. Stevenson replied. She looked like she was about to say something else but then just gave him a tight smile instead. "Have a good one!"

"Thanks!"

He turned and left the classroom. Adam and Jenn were still within view down the hall.

"Psst! Guys!" Ted called. "Wait up!"

They turned and waited, greeting him with grins.

"How you feeling, Steady Teddy?"

"Pretty great," Ted admitted. "I thought I'd

feel guilty right now, but I'm mostly just happy to be out of there."

As he said it, Ted knew it was true. Adrenaline was pumping through his veins, the good kind this time, and he felt great. It was exhilarating. If Nina wasn't still back there taking her test for real, he would probably go right up to her and ask for her phone number.

"We should celebrate," said Adam. "Want to hit the vending machine before second period starts?"

"Sounds like a plan," Ted replied.

"Dude, you have gym class next period," said Jenn. "Won't soda make you feel nasty?"

Ted shook his head and smiled. "Now that the test is out of the way, nasty isn't even in my vocabulary."

* * *

Long after he finished the last of his soda from the vending machine, Ted could still taste victory as he sat in English class later that afternoon. He couldn't tell if it was the sugar or the rush of getting away with what he had done, but he felt almost giddy as he sat through another group discussion with the theater kids.

"So anyways," said Rosie, "I just thought that line from Friar Lawrence—'these violent delights have violent ends'—was just perfect for describing the whole play. Every time Romeo or Juliet get anything to be happy about, something tragic happens to balance it. Everything evens out."

"Um, yeah," said Fred. "The play is called a tragedy for a reason."

Rosie crossed her arms.

"I think she has a point," said Ted.

They both looked at him, surprised.

"It's all about balance and change, like in nature. There are all these lines in the play about plants and stuff"—he flipped through his copy of the play—"like here, 'this bud of love.' Maybe that could be a part of it. Buds turn into flowers, you know? Plants are always growing and changing. Nothing ever stays the same for long, even if you like it the way it is. Romeo and Juliet can't seem to hang onto a good streak because that's not how life works. Like it or not, things will keep changing."

Fred and Rosie gaped at him.

"Are you feeling okay?" asked Fred. "No offense, I've just never seen you this awake and, like, trying."

"Yeah," said Rosie, leaning forward. "Also, that was awesome."

Ted shrugged and smiled. "Thanks. I guess I'm just having an awesome day."

Before either of them could respond, there was a knock on the classroom door. One of the school administrators stepped into the room.

"Ted Cooper?"

The class went silent.

Maybe I was a little hasty on the awesome day thing, Ted thought.

He swallowed. "Um, yeah. That's me."

"You're wanted in the principal's office, son."

"Oooh," someone murmured.

Rosie slowly leaned back in her chair. "Looks like you couldn't hang onto your good streak either," she whispered.

Ted felt his face flush, but he did his best to do a casual, non-committal shrug.

I really don't know what you're talking about, pal, but I'll go to the office with you, said his shrug. *I am not panicking because I haven't done anything wrong.*

I'm panicking, said his brain.

Ted stood, feeling everyone's eyes on his back. He shuffled his papers into his backpack and followed the administrator out of the room.

* * *

When Ted opened the door to Principal Blueman's office, Ms. Stevenson was standing by the desk, arms crossed. She didn't look at him.

Three green fabric chairs were lined up in front of her. In one, Adam was staring stonily down at his feet. In the other, Jenn was bobbing her leg, a nervous habit he'd thought she had kicked back in sixth grade.

Ted had never been called to the principal's office before, which was a good thing, but that also meant he had no idea what to do. His mind lurched, struggling to process what was before him.

"Oh good, you're all here," Principal Blueman boomed from the doorway behind him.

Ted turned.

"Have a seat, Ted."

He sat.

Principal Blueman circled around the line of chairs to reach his desk, dropping into his own chair with a thud.

"Do the three of you," he said, clasping his huge hands together, "know why you're here?"

No one said a word.

Principal Blueman sighed. "Well, then, Ms. Stevenson, why don't you just tell them what you told me?"

"I thought it was odd," Ms. Stevenson began, "that three students had finished the unit test early. One or two is normal for this group, but three just doesn't usually happen."

Ted bit his lip.

This is my fault, he thought.

"So," Ms. Stevenson continued, "I was

curious. I took a look at your tests while the rest of the class finished up. You all got a forty-nine out of fifty, and you all missed question eighteen."

Ted tried to keep his chin from trembling.

She's right, he thought. *I should have remembered that. I completely forgot. We're getting caught because of me.*

"What are the odds of that, in your experience?" rumbled Principal Blueman.

Ms. Stevenson paused. "Low."

Principal Blueman leaned forward in his chair. "We take cheating very seriously. There are going to be consequences."

Jenn looked pale. "Am I going to be kicked off of the soccer team?"

Principal Blueman sighed. "No, Jennifer. You can still play on the team."

"Are you going to tell our parents?" asked Adam.

Ms. Stevenson nodded.

"Your parents have all gotten phone calls explaining what happened and that the three of you will be doing an in-school suspension tomorrow," said Principal Blueman. "We will also send you home with a letter for your parents to sign."

Ted slumped back in his chair. Dinner that night was going to be bad.

* * *

Ted was wrong. Dinner wasn't bad—it was horrible.

His mom came home just at Ted finished making pasta. "Hey, Mom, how was your day?" he asked, trying to sound casual. But he was too jittery to pull it off.

"I got a voicemail from the school. It said that you got an in-school suspension tomorrow because you cheated on your history test," she said quietly. She looked down at him. "Teddy . . . is that really true? Did you cheat?"

Ted swallowed hard. He tried to think of something to say, something to make it sound less bad, but he came up with nothing.

"I'm so sorry, Mom."

His mom didn't sigh, exactly, but she seemed to deflate a little, and as Ted scanned her face for her reaction, he noticed how truly tired she looked.

There were delicate blue circles showing through the makeup under his mom's eyes, and a piece of her hair was stuck to the edge of her temple. She looked utterly worn out. Shaking her head, his mom sat down, picked up her fork, and took a slow bite of pasta.

That silence from his mom was the worst thing. Worse than the long lecture that eventually followed. Worse than being grounded and told he couldn't go to Adam's piano recital tomorrow night, to the diner afterward, or to Jenn's soccer game on Saturday. Worse, even, than getting caught cheating.

* * *

Ted's eyes blurred with tears as he climbed the stairs up to his room. He slammed the door behind him, did a running jump into his bed, and rolled himself up in his blankets like the world's most upset burrito.

How, he thought, *did things manage to get so much worse?*

He pulled out his phone and tried to find the do-over text message.

I need a do-over for this do-over, he thought, wiping his burning cheeks.

But instead, it looked like he was going to have to live with the choice he'd made this time around.

I, Ted Cooper, am a cheat, he thought right before drifting off.

6

One fitful night of sleep and one tense car ride later, Ted found himself back at school the next morning—it was Thursday, he had checked—an hour earlier than usual for his first-ever in-school suspension.

Ted never thought he would be happy to be at school, or anywhere, early. Today, though, Ted was glad that the halls were empty. Everything was terrible, but at least nobody would know he was going to in-school suspension.

Then again, he realized, the whole girls' soccer team would notice that Jenn wouldn't be at practice that morning, and she was probably going to tell them why. From there, the information would spread through the rest of the school by noon. Nina would definitely hear about it.

Ted signed in at the front office, writing his name on a clipboard right under Jenn and Adam's names. A school secretary led him down the hall and into a small classroom he had never been in before.

The first thing he noticed about the classroom was that there were no windows. The bumpy cinder-block walls, painted with thin white paint, pressed in around three lines of desks.

Adam sat cross-armed at one of the desks, below a poster with a floppy-eared dog on it and the words *Are you in trouble? Don't worry. Even an old dog can learn new tricks!*

From the stony expression on his face, Adam was not interested in learning new tricks. Adam had texted them the bad news that morning: he was grounded too. He wouldn't be going to the diner after his recital.

Jenn sat at the desk next to his, looking almost as grumpy as Adam. She hated when plans fell through. She gave Ted a quick nod hello and then continued staring at the ceiling.

Ted slid into the desk behind hers.

"Your in-school suspension will begin once I read you the following," said the school secretary. She took out a folder and began to repeat the rules listed in the letter the school had sent home with them for their parents the day before.

"The students will stay in their seats at all times and work on their classwork. They are not allowed to sleep, to use their phones, to listen to music, to speak to each other, or to leave this room. A teacher or staff member will check in every so often to make sure the students are following the rules and to escort students to the bathroom for bathroom breaks as needed. You will be dismissed at three o'clock this afternoon." She looked up from the folder. "Do you all have your packed lunches?"

Ted, Adam, and Jenn all nodded.

"Good," said the school secretary. "Hand me your phones, please. I'll return them at the end of the day." When they'd turned over their phones, she turned and left the room, letting the door bang shut behind her.

Silence settled over the cramped room like a heavy fog.

Ted tried not to think about how loud his breath sounded. He opened his science homework and tried to use up all of his brain cells learning about cells.

The clock on the classroom wall was broken—bored to death, Ted guessed, just like everyone else who'd had to sit through in-school suspension there—and they weren't allowed to use their phones, so there was no way to know how much time was passing.

Sometime in the mid-morning, there was a knock on the door. Ted looked up and saw Ms. Stevenson open it and step into the room.

Ted realized he had never seen her look anything but happy. She did not look happy today.

"Hi. I just came in to check on you three," Ms. Stevenson said in a quiet voice. "Do you need anything?"

Adam, Jenn, and Ted all shook their heads no.

"Okay," Ms. Stevenson said. She paused. "I have to say, I am really disappointed that you guys cheated. You are all such bright kids. Even if you didn't get the grade you wanted, it would have been so much better if you had just tried your best." She looked down at her feet. "I don't know. I just wish you had talked to me if you were having trouble. I wish you would had believed in yourselves as much as I believe in you."

She looked at them, and Ted felt himself getting misty all over again.

"I'm really sorry," he whispered.

"Thank you, Ted." Ms. Stevenson rubbed the side of her face and then sighed. "I teach history because it's important to learn from our past mistakes. I really hope the three of you will learn from this one."

She turned and left.

Ted let his forehead sink to the desk. His eyes stung.

Don't cry, he thought. *Do not even think about crying. You are the worst person ever and she is so nice and that was devastating, but don't you dare even think about—*

Jenn snorted.

Ted raised his head. "What?"

"Can you believe her?" Jenn said with a sneer. "'I wish,'" she repeated in a high-pitched voice, "'you would have believed in yourselves as much as I believe in you.'"

Adam chuckled. "That was straight out of some cheesy movie."

"And she teaches history because it's important to"—Jenn made air quotes with her hands—"'learn from our past mistakes?' It was her mistake to leave the answers out in the first place."

Adam nodded. "They were just sitting there in full view, and now she's all high and mighty? What a joke."

"Guys," Ted said, "come on, lay off."

Jenn rolled her eyes. "Seriously, Ted. That was so weird."

"No, but actually, though," said Ted. "You shouldn't be so hard on her." He took a deep breath. "And, for the record, I think she's right. What we did was a mistake. We've been real jerks."

Jenn's lip twitched.

"Whoa there," Adam joked, putting his hands up in the air. "We're sorry. We didn't realize we were in the presence of Sir Teddy, knight in shining armor for high school history teachers."

"Should Nina be worried about this new crush?" asked Jenn.

"Knock it off, guys."

"If you wanted to get Ms. Stevenson's attention, you didn't have to go to all of this trouble," said Adam.

Jenn laughed. "Ted and Ms. Stevenson, sitting in a tree—"

"Ew, stop. Are you in second grade?" snapped Ted. "This is serious."

"No, you stop," said Jenn. "We didn't force you to cheat with us. You asked for the answers, remember?"

Ted exhaled and looked up at the gray-speckled ceiling. "Well, I shouldn't have."

"Yeah, but you did!" said Adam, raising his voice.

"Yeah, and now I realize it was a bad call!"

Ted retorted. "All it did was hurt people and get us in trouble. None of us should have done it."

"Enough!" Jenn shouted. "You can mope about it and blame us if you want, but that's your problem. Seriously, all you do is whine about things that are your own fault. Oh, I'm not ready for the test, even though I don't have any extracurricular activities getting in the way of studying, wah wah. Oh, I can't get Nina Alvarez's number, even though I've never bothered to say a single word to her so that I could actually get to know her. Oh, I got caught cheating, even though I chose to do it—"

The classroom door burst open. The school secretary's eyes were wide behind her wire-rimmed glasses. "The students are not allowed to speak to each other," she hissed. "This is your first warning. The next time that we have to tell you to keep quiet in here, we will add another half hour of in-school suspension."

"Thanks a lot, Sir Teddy," Adam said under his breath.

The school secretary put a finger to her lips. "Shush! That is enough from the three of you." She glared at each of them and then left the room again.

No one spoke.

Ted stared up at the dog poster above Jenn's head. Sitting in that classroom, he felt like he was locked in a kennel—with two bigger, meaner dogs. He hadn't thought about Adam and Jenn as mean before, just as two smart and sarcastic people with whom he was lucky to be friends. Now . . . the way they acted just felt different. Ugly.

Maybe not being on their level isn't such a bad thing, thought Ted.

It wasn't that he didn't want to be friends with them. He still did. They were his best friends, after all. He couldn't picture going through the school day without joking around with them in class or at lunch . . . but maybe it was time to think about making other friends too.

It just felt like he had seen another side of them—and Ted didn't like what he saw. He didn't want to be like that. The way the school secretary had just looked at them, though—it was as if they were all the same.

He had to do something. He had to make things right somehow. Adam and Jenn clearly weren't interested—whatever Ted did, he knew he would have to do by himself. He could think about his social life later. Right now, he just needed to fix this mess.

Ted tapped a pen against his temple.

Think, Ted. Think. What are you good at? Besides messing things up and sleeping . . .

Then he looked at the pen.

Bingo.

* * *

When he got out of in-school suspension that afternoon, Ted biked home faster than he had moved all year. He thundered upstairs to his bedroom and took out his gold rush history notes, his textbook, an old box of art supplies, and a stack of blank paper from the printer in his mom's home office.

He spread it all out across his desk and peered down at it with the intensity and importance of a general with a table full of maps. After a minute or so, he picked up a pen and began to trace a thin black line down one of the pieces of paper.

Ted's phone buzzed twice in his pocket. He pulled it out and tossed it over onto his bed, barely registering the texts on the screen from the group chat.

He knew the texts were probably from Adam and Jenn, hopefully apologizing for their fight. But right now, Ted didn't really want to hear what they had to say.

He was so focused on what was unfolding in front of him on the paper that the knock on his bedroom door almost startled him out of his chair.

His mom pushed the door halfway open.

"May I come in?" she asked.

He nodded.

Ted's mom stepped into the room, taking in the pile of dirty clothes by his hamper, a forgotten glass of water on his nightstand, and the stack of items in front of him on the desk. She moved his phone aside and sat down on the unmade bed.

"More penguins?"

"Huh?" asked Ted.

She lifted her chin in the direction of the paper on the desk. "Are you drawing more penguins, like you did the other day?"

Right, thought Ted. *That penguin I drew on the napkin.*

He felt like that had happened years ago, not days.

He spun in his desk chair, hiding the paper from view behind his back. "It's, um, something I'm working on for school."

His mom looked like she wanted to ask another question, but she just pressed her lips together and looked down.

"For my history class," Ted added.

When his mom looked back up at him, Ted thought he saw a muscle in her face soften.

"That's great, Teddy."

"I should probably get back to work on it," said Ted. "Do you need anything?"

His mom paused, and then shook her head. "No. I was just came in to see how you were doing. It's . . . it's nice to see you so hard at work on a school project."

"Thanks, Mom. I'm fine."

She stood up. "I'll leave you to it. Come downstairs when you feel hungry. I'm about to order a pizza."

"Sounds good," Ted replied, already swiveling back around in his chair. "Thanks."

He picked up the green marker and kept drawing.

The next morning, Ted was up and dressed
before his alarm went off.

He couldn't remember the last time he
had been this awake this early. He felt like
he was seeing the world through a morning
person's eyes for the first time in his life.
The pens and papers were splayed across
his desk the way he had left them the night
before, and the floorboards still squeaked the
way they always did when he went to brush
his teeth, but the light coming in through
the windows was paler, and the world was
quiet. Peaceful.

On the ride to school, Ted held his backpack

in his lap with what he had finished the night before tucked inside.

His mom bobbed her head to the music playing over the car radio.

Thankfully, this time it was some song Ted didn't know. They must have hired someone new at the radio station.

"I didn't hear you go to bed last night," his mom said after the last chorus had ended. "How late did you stay up?"

"I don't really know," Ted admitted. "It was pretty late, though."

"My kid?" his mom asked, surprised. She turned the radio off. "Up late and then up early?"

"Yeah, I don't know," said Ted, shrugging. "I was pretty much just in the zone until I finished my project."

"So it would seem," his mom said, raising her eyebrows as they reached a red light. "Are you going to let me see this mystery project of yours?"

Ted paused, then nodded. He unzipped his backpack, pulled the project out, and handed it to her.

His mom took it, carefully. The minivan engine hummed as she flipped through each of the pages.

"Oh, Teddy."

Ted looked up at her and saw her face brightening with the first real smile he'd seen in days.

"Is that a good 'oh, Teddy' or a bad 'oh, Teddy?'" he asked.

"It's good. You've done an incredible job."

She handed Ted back his project, and he put it back in his bag as the light turned green again.

"Do you think she'll like it?" asked Ted.

"I don't know, kiddo," his mom replied. "I can only speak for me." She checked the rearview mirror. "Speaking for me, though, I think it might help."

"You do?"

"I do," said his mom. "You can't change what you did—"

Not again, anyway, thought Ted.

"But you can show her that you care, and that your heart is in the right place, even if your brain wasn't," she said, shooting him a look. "That might not go a long way with her, but it certainly does with me."

They pulled up in front of the school.

Ted turned to her and, letting his backpack fall to his feet, leaned over and gave his mom a huge hug.

"Thank you so much, Mom. I love you."

"I love you too, Teddy."

"I promise never to do this again."

She smiled down at him and ruffled his hair. "Good. Now get out there and make this right, or as close to right as you can."

"I'll try."

* * *

Ted's early start meant that Jenn and Adam were not yet in their usual places—they weren't waiting by the front door of the school, and when he glanced down the hall at Jenn's locker he didn't see them there either.

He couldn't tell if he felt relieved or not. He had to admit, though, it was weird not seeing them.

Ted took the long way to the history classroom. He passed the door once, and then looped back around to get a sip of water from the drinking fountain before class. As he bent down to the spigot, he felt someone's eyes on the back of his head.

Turning, he saw Nina waiting for a turn at the fountain. *Okay. Be cool, Ted*, he thought. *Everything is fine.* Ordinarily, he would've awkwardly shuffled aside without saying a word. But today he decided to try something new. "Hey, Nina," he said. "How's it going?"

She looked surprised—which was understandable since he'd never spoken to her before. "Uh, hey, Ted. Just gonna get a drink of water."

"Right. Of course. All yours."

He stepped out her way, his whole body humming with nervous tension. *Okay, that didn't go so bad—*

"Have you been sick? I noticed you weren't in class yesterday."

Nina Alvarez had noticed him? Or at least the absence of him? This was a breakthrough.

Or would've been, under different circumstances.

"Uh, yeah, I . . ." Somehow she must not have heard what had really happened. It occurred to him that he could easily lie—say he'd had a stomach bug or something—but he didn't want his first-ever conversation with Nina to be a dishonest one. Instead he said, "Yeah, I got an in-school suspension for cheating on the history test. Not my proudest moment."

Nina pursed her lips. "Seriously? You cheated in Stevenson's class? That's so messed up."

"Agreed," he said. "Temporary lapse of judgment. But I'm a changed man now."

"Okaaaaay," Nina said. "Whatever." She leaned down to take a gulp of water, and Ted realized she was probably done talking to him.

"Well, see you in class," he said with an awkward wave, turning to head off down the hallway. He exhaled and ran his hands through his hair.

All right, he thought. *That was awkward and embarrassing, but I guess I deserved it.*

* * *

Following in twos and threes, his classmates entered the room and took their seats. Ted drew a vine snaking around the edge of his notebook. His hands were clammy on his pencil as he watched the door, half-hoping that Adam and Jenn would show up and half-hoping that they wouldn't.

Just before the bell rang, the door swung open. Adam and Jenn strolled in, laughing about something.

Ted tried to swallow the lump of jealousy in his throat when he saw that they had matching bottles of iced tea from the vending machine.

They sat down.

"Good morning, everyone, and happy Friday!" said Ms. Stevenson. "Please open your textbooks to chapter five."

Ted felt a soft poke on his back, and then a folded paper square landed in front of him on his desk.

He opened it.

You didn't answer my texts last night, read the note in Adam's handwriting. *Fighting with you feels weird. We lost our cool and said some messed up things. We were embarrassed that we got caught cheating, and we shouldn't have taken that out on you. Can we rewind and skip what happened?*

The corner of Ted's mouth twitched. Going back and changing things hadn't exactly been a winning strategy in the last few days.

Ted stared down at the paper, thinking. Then he pressed his pen to the paper and drew a little remote with just one button, which he decorated with two small triangles.

Thanks for apologizing. We can't really go back, he wrote, *but I think we can probably get past it. If you promise to go easier on me and other people, we could fast forward to things being cool again. If you want.*

He tossed the note back over his shoulder.

After a minute or two, Adam flicked it back onto Ted's desk.

Deal, Adam had written. *I'm going to pay attention now. Oh, and don't worry about Jenn. She's stubborn, but she'll come around.*

Well, thought Ted, *she's not the first person to be mad at me this week.*

He glanced over to his left, at Jenn's desk.

She stared at her paper, taking notes on what Ms. Stevenson was saying. It was a safe bet that there would be no folded paper squares coming from her direction.

At the front of the room, Ms. Stevenson pointed to a map of the United States.

"We really can't talk about this time period without talking about railroads," Ms. Stevenson continued. "In fact, the California gold rush helped pay for the western part of the first transcontinental railroad. Now that California was connected to folks here in the middle of the country, as well as out east . . ."

Ted leaned over slightly. "Five bucks says this unit is on track to go better than the last one," he whispered.

Jenn rolled her eyes. "Really, Ted?"

Ted waggled his eyebrows. "You're not all aboard for train-based humor?"

She tried to hide a half smile. "This just really isn't the . . . platform for it."

"If the two of you don't shut up," Adam whispered, "I'm going to lose my train of thought back here."

Jenn chuckled.

They tuned back in to what Ms. Stevenson was saying, taking notes in a comfortable silence instead of an awkward one.

Ted smiled, feeling almost happy again. Almost. There was still one more thing that he had to do.

* * *

History class ended. Adam and Jenn put their things in their backpacks and stood, ready to leave.

"Why aren't you packing up, Ted?" Jenn asked.

"I'm going to stay back, actually," said Ted. "I just have to take care of something. I can catch up with you afterward."

"All right," Jenn said with a shrug. "We'll see you later."

He waited until most of the other students had left the classroom and then went up to the front of the room with his open backpack.

Ms. Stevenson was quietly reshuffling papers on her desk.

She sighed and looked up. "Is there something I can help you with, Ted?"

"I, um, just wanted you to know that I thought about what you said yesterday, about history and learning from your past mistakes."

Ms. Stevenson looked surprised. "You did?"

Ted nodded and then took a deep breath. "Cheating on the test was a mistake. I was having trouble with this unit, and I was embarrassed about it, but I should have just come to you for help. I know I let you down. You have been nothing but nice and helpful, and I blew it. I'm not great at a lot of things, but I . . . I really like to draw. I know this doesn't make up for what I did, and it can't, but I looked over the notes that I had and I made this last night to show you that I do care, and that I'm really sorry."

He took another deep breath and handed her what he had made.

"The Misadventures of Fred: A California Gold Rush Story," Ms. Stevenson read out loud from the front cover. She looked back down at him. "You made this last night?"

He nodded. "It's a comic book about, um, a California gold rush prospector named Fred. He's also based on the material for the test. Basically, he hears about gold out in California and he decides to go out there and try to strike it rich. He convinces his wife to help him sell most of their stuff so that he can afford the trip. He promises to find a ton of gold, get rich, and then send for her and their kids. But, just like we talked about in class, by the time he gets to California, there isn't a lot of gold left for him to easily find. He gets stuck there, and he doesn't know what to do."

Ms. Stevenson opened the comic book. "Oh my," she whispered.

He watched her take in the panels of Fred, with a big brown hat and a round belly held in place by mining trousers and suspenders.

Ms. Stevenson's fingers paused on the panel on the next page where Fred, thin and leathery from long days in the sun, finally sat down in his tent under the California stars and wrote a letter to his wife.

"Fred makes a mistake, owns up to it,

and then makes the best out of the situation," said Ted. He shifted his weight from one foot to the other. "That's what I want to do, Ms. Stevenson. I know my grade is basically in the toilet now, and I deserve that, but from here on out I just want you to know that I'm going to do my best."

"Ted," said Ms. Stevenson, "I'm touched." She turned another page of the comic book, shaking her head slowly. "You clearly put a lot of effort into this. The art is fantastic, and I can tell that you drew on what we talked about in class. These details . . . I mean, just look at the pan Fred uses when he goes panning for gold . . . and these masts in the ships stranded in the San Francisco harbor." Her eyes widened. "Oh, and look at the buttons on those Levi Strauss mining trousers! This is really wonderful."

Ted didn't realize he was holding his breath. "Thank you, Ms. Stevenson."

"No, Ted, thank you." She flipped the comic book closed and clasped it to her chest. "I wasn't planning on doing this . . . but I think you have earned it. How would you feel about a do-over?"

Ted nearly dropped his backpack.

"Another chance, I mean," said Ms. Stevenson. "To save your grade. I can't give you an actual do-over of the unit test—the school policy on cheating says that I still have to give you a zero on that—but you could at least take it again to earn some extra credit." She smiled. "What do you say? Here at lunch on Monday?"

Ted grinned. "I say thank you. That sounds awesome. I'll be there."

"You're welcome, Ted. Thank you again for this comic book." She paused. "I'd like to show this to the school art club, if that's all right with you."

"We have an art club?"

Ms. Stevenson nodded. "I'm the staff sponsor. I'm surprised you aren't in it, actually. You should think about joining us. We meet on Tuesday afternoons after school."

The warning bell for second-period classes rang.

"I need to get ready for my next class now," said Ms. Stevenson, "but I can ask the art club student president to tell you more about the club, if you'd like. It's Nina Alvarez—she actually sits a few rows ahead of you in class."

He gulped. "Um, yeah. I would like that very much." Maybe he could start fresh with Nina too. Maybe knowing that they had something in common would make it easier for him to talk to her—actually get to know her, like Jenn had said.

Behind him, the seats were filling with a second round of history students.

"You should go get ready for your next class, too, Ted," Ms. Stevenson said, gently.

"Oh, right," he replied. "Yeah, I should get to gym. I'll see you on Monday!"

Ted stepped out into the hall, standing a little straighter and feeling a little lighter than he had before. He could barely believe it. He was going to actually get to know Nina, and he was going to get a do-over of the test—a real do-over, one that he had earned, not gotten from some weird text.

Maybe, Ted thought, *the best second chances are the ones you make for yourself.*

He floated down the hall, picturing the look on his mom's face when he told her about the test. Picturing spending his Tuesdays drawing with Nina and Ms. Stevenson. Picturing hanging out with Jenn and Adam.

The locker room was empty when he got there; everyone had already gotten dressed and gone out to the field for class.

Ted barely noticed. He changed into his gym clothes as if he were in a daze and then headed outside.

It was a beautiful October morning. Sunlight streamed down over the field and everyone on it, as bright and clear as what lay ahead of him. Ted smiled.

He wouldn't change a thing.

« ABOUT THE AUTHOR

SARAH RICHMAN is a writer, author, and poet based in Washington, D.C. Her work is published in literary magazines and reviews across the United States and Scotland. She likes good tea and bad jokes. To learn more about Sarah, visit sarahrichmanwriter.com.

THE DO-OVER

THE ACCIDENT
THE CHEAT
THE DATE
THE GAME
THE LIE
THE PRANK

ATTACK ON EARTH

WHEN ALIENS INVADE, ALL YOU CAN DO IS SURVIVE.

DESERTED

THE FALLOUT

THE FIELD TRIP

GETTING HOME

LOCKDOWN

TAKE SHELTER

CHECK OUT ALL THE TITLES IN THE
ATTACK ON EARTH SERIES

SUPER HUMAN

HAVING A SUPERPOWER IS NOT AS EASY AS THE COMIC BOOKS MAKE IT SEEM.

SUPER HUMAN — MIND OVER MATTER — R. T. MARTIN

SUPER HUMAN — NOW YOU SEE ME — VANESSA ACTON

SUPER HUMAN — PICKING UP SPEED — RAELYN DRAKE

SUPER HUMAN — STRETCHED TOO THIN — RAELYN DRAKE

SUPER HUMAN — STRONGHOLD — R. T. MARTIN

SUPER HUMAN — TAKE TO THE SKIES — R. T. MARTIN